HE'S BACK!

Though he'll never make the ten-best-dressed list or win a Nobel Prize, Herman's back, looking at life as only he can.

"Apart from a little dampness, Herman, how's everything else?"

More Big Laughs from SIGNET

"Apart from a little dampness, Herman, how's everything else?"

by Jim Unger

A SIGNET BOOK
NEW AMERICAN LIBRARY
PUBLISHED BY
THE NEW AMERICAN LIBRARY
OF CANADA LIMITED

First Signet Printing, February 1984

   2 3 4 5 6 7 8 9

"I think I'll take just ONE of these!"

"Testing...testing...one, two, three."

"Whadyer mean the needle's broken off?"

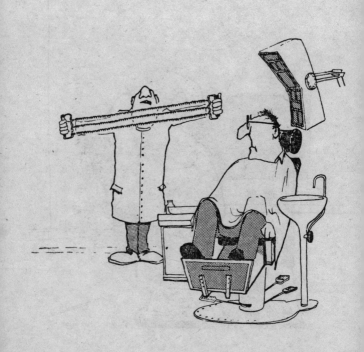

"Can't you cook yourself something when I'm out?"

"He's doing two weeks 'solitary'!"

"If I lose . . . the bet's off, okay?"

"I can imagine the fuss you'd make if I walked
around dressed like that!"

"Okay...here's the results of your medical."

"Whadyer mean we don't need any brushes?"

"How many times have I told you to wear
your helmet?"

"You're using my athlete's foot ointment."

"What was that?"

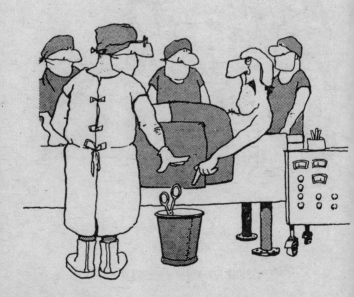

"Pity . . . would've made a nice set of luggage."

EGGS

EXTRA LARGE

"I think I'm gonna need a couple of days off sick!"

"Father, I cannot tell a lie...

Muhammad Ali did it."

"This year I'm gonna finish off the basement!"

"You spotted it, eh?"

"It says right here on the can, 'Do not use
to clean overnight .' "

"They think of everything...that's in case
you forget your key."

"Okay, you wanna play rough...gimme the
beads back!"

"Your mother just phoned...she's
coming over."

"It doesn't matter what sort of dog you've got,
   . . . it's guaranteed to keep away burglars."

"Mind if we play through?"

"This self-adjusting set is giving me the creeps!"

"Don't look at me...you gave him the
carpentry set."

"Two weeks of jogging and so far he's made the front door."

"They've cured my arthritis!"

"Okay class...name four things he did wrong."

"You must be the new member."

"Herman, I can see perfectly well without a chair
to stand on . . . Herman!!!"

"Now whatever happens, hang on to those sandwiches!"

"Hey! Is there another word for 'Verily' that starts with a 'B'?"

"A-B-C-E . . . G."

"So what happened when you called him an idiot?"

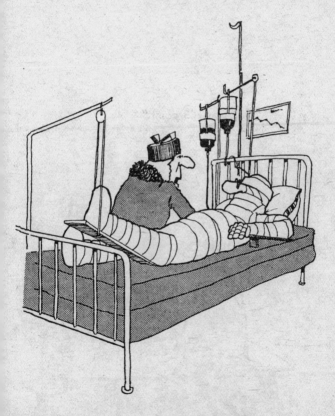

"Your boss says you can have the rest of
the afternoon off . . ."

"That was HIS point."

"Herman, your Doctor told you to
get away and RELAX."

"Has he had his dinner?"

"She doesn't buy many luxuries but
she loves her stereo."

"Will you quit shouting 'land on the starboard beam,' while we're in port!"

"Take it easy with him, his wife just had triplets."

"You go across the square, pass the nurse's residence, up the steps, through the main lobby...and second door on your left."

"Okay, you can go now . . . they've evacuated the village."

"Here...make a wish."

"You've got a nice little recession of your own going on up here!"

"I don't want to ruin your day Herman but
tomorrow morning I want to see you in my office."

"D'yer ever feel you're on the verge of
an incredible breakthrough?"

"No I don't know what sort it is but all my instincts tell me we should be about forty miles away when it hatches."

"I just spent $8,000 having this room soundproofed."

"Forgive the intrusion...I wonder if you'd mind telling the janitor the elevator's stuck?"

"Nice work Spike, you've hurt his arm."

"This model comes with shoulder straps for canoe trips, etc."

"What do you think?...If it's gonna take six hours to wear off, shall we send out for a pizza?"

"Starting tomorrow I don't want you to wash the 5,000 year old jugs!"

"Herman, will you stop fooling around and finish cleaning these windows."

"Why doesn't he throw it at the one who cooks it?"

"Take your time Doc. I'm enjoying reading
'Predictions for 1948.'"

"What'sa matter with that goofy cat?"

"Can you remember where I bought this suit?"

"Herman, don't go too far you'll miss Gunsmoke."

**I want you to know there's nothing
personal in this!"**

"You can't claim a world record unless it sticks
in the grass."

"Here comes this week's challenge!"

"You can believe what you like . . . I tell
you I saw one!"

"I think he wants to be friends!"

"I'll give you two clues . . . we get Wild Kingdom
on every channel and the cat's missing."

"At a time when everyone's supposed to be
conserving energy...you're certainly doing your bit."

"Imagine those crooks wanting
eleven bucks to fix this!"

"Now do you believe me Herman? . . . is that a
sand-trap or is that a sand-trap?"

"Nice try!"

"Herman, this is our deluxe comfort model."

"Oh he hasn't escaped...he just gets these sudden cravings for a cheeseburger."

"Let me put it this way . . . for your weight you should be thirty-seven feet tall."

"Anybody got the right time?"

"This toaster's gotta go back!"

"Do we need a set of encyclopedias?"

"Herman's so considerate when I'm sick...brought
the washer and dryer up to the bedroom."

"How about a ten-minute 'shore-leave' to take out the garbage?"

"Next door wants 'The Blue Danube.'"

"He's always the same when we go camping . . .
wakes up and can't remember where he is."

"Second serve."

"You told me to use my initiative if I needed
money, so I sold your car."

"Try again, sir; that was my foot."

ABOUT THE AUTHOR

JIM UNGER was born in London, England. After surviving the blitz bombings of World War II, and two years in the British Army, followed by a short career as a London bobby and a driving instructor, he immigrated to Canada in 1968 and became a newspaper graphic artist and editorial cartoonist. For three years running he won the Ontario Weekly Newspaper Association's "Cartoonist of the Year" award. In 1974 he began drawing HERMAN for the Universal Press Syndicate, with instant popularity. HERMAN is now enjoyed by 60 million daily and Sunday newspaper readers all around the world. His cartoon collections, THE HERMAN TREASURIES, became paperback bestsellers.

Jim Unger now lives in Nassau, Bahamas.